America,
My New Home

America, My New Home

Poems by **Monica Gunning**

Illustrations by **Ken Condon**

WORDSONG

Honesdale, Pennsylvania

To my grandson Mark Gunning
—M. G.

To Memere, a tough woman with a soft heart. Also to my loving and
supportive family. Thank you, Caroline, Jeannine, and Mom
—K. C.

Text copyright © 2004 by Monica Gunning
Illustrations copyright © 2004 by Ken Condon
All rights reserved

Wordsong
An Imprint of Boyds Mills Press, Inc.
A Highlights Company
815 Church Street
Honesdale, Pennsylvania 18431
Printed in China

Library of Congress Cataloging-in-Publication Data

Gunning, Monica.
America, my new home : poems / by Monica Gunning ; illustrations by Ken Condon.— 1st ed.
p.   cm.
ISBN 978-1-59078-057-2 (alk. paper)
1. Children's poetry, American. 2. United States—Juvenile poetry.
3. Emigration and immigration—Juvenile poetry. 4. Jamaican
Americans—Juvenile poetry. 5. Immigrants—Juvenile poetry. 6. Jamaica—Juvenile poetry.
[1. Jamaican Americans—Poetry. 2. Emigration and immigration—Poetry. 3. Immigrants—Poetry.
4. Jamaica—Poetry. 5. American poetry.]
I. Condon, Ken, ill. II. Title.
PR9205.9.G86A46 2004
811'.54—dc22
2003026870

First edition, 2004
The text of this book is set in 13-point Electra.

www.boydsmillspress.com

10 9 8 7 6 5 4 3

Contents

America, My New Home

A new country,
far from my Jamaica sea foam;
waves of people,
new sights, bright lights—
America, my new home.

Statue of Liberty

Standing
with her torch high,
the lady welcomes me
to step on freedom's soil and live
my dreams.

Skyscrapers

Sky-high climbers
brace against
winter's cold
in drab gray coats
until their lights
go on at night,
millions of
sparkling eyes—
these giants outdazzle
even the stars.

Wide-Awake City

When night shadows
sneak about,
one by one
village lights flicker out.
Only sparkling stars
stay shiny bright;
or the moon casts
a pale floodlight
in the country dark.
My village sleeps.

My new city
electrifies the night.
Skyscraper windows
glimmer silvery white.
Neon lights blink
hello good-bye.
Traffic,
a glowing serpentine,
winds in a city
wide awake, all night.

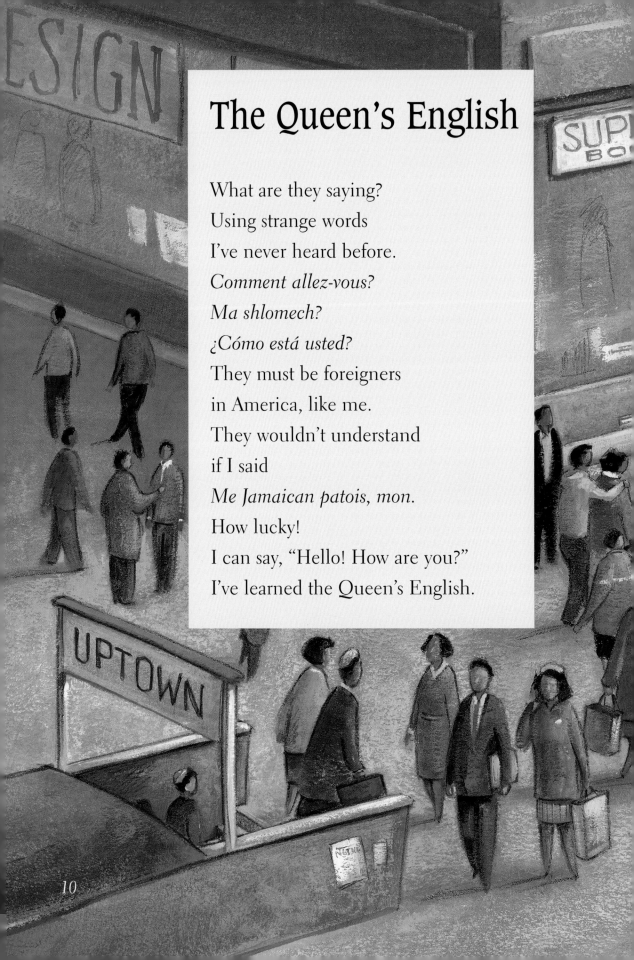

The Queen's English

What are they saying?
Using strange words
I've never heard before.
Comment allez-vous?
Ma shlomech?
¿Cómo está usted?
They must be foreigners
in America, like me.
They wouldn't understand
if I said
Me Jamaican patois, mon.
How lucky!
I can say, "Hello! How are you?"
I've learned the Queen's English.

Why Such a Hurry?

Back home in the village,
no one was in a hurry
to catch a bus or train.
There were none for which to scurry.

People rode their horses or mules,
had time to say hello.
Many walked to work; except
in flurries of rain, the pace was slow.

Why such a hurry here
to catch a bus or train?
Did so many sleep too late?
And I see no signs of rain.

No One Knows My Name

When I walked
down the road,
I'd hear Aunt Sue's voice,
"How you doing, dear heart?"
Or "There goes me sunshine girl!"
Uncle Joe would call from his cart.

Here in the big city,
thousands pass me by.
I'm one more unknown face.
No sweet voices like rain
sprinkle me with care.
No one knows or calls my name.

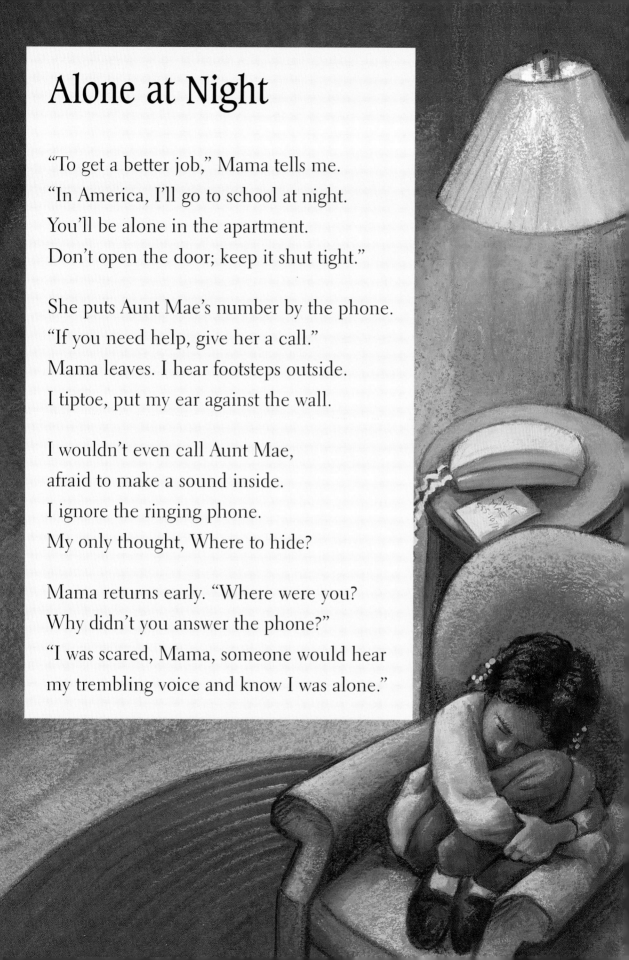

Alone at Night

"To get a better job," Mama tells me.
"In America, I'll go to school at night.
You'll be alone in the apartment.
Don't open the door; keep it shut tight."

She puts Aunt Mae's number by the phone.
"If you need help, give her a call."
Mama leaves. I hear footsteps outside.
I tiptoe, put my ear against the wall.

I wouldn't even call Aunt Mae,
afraid to make a sound inside.
I ignore the ringing phone.
My only thought, Where to hide?

Mama returns early. "Where were you?
Why didn't you answer the phone?"
"I was scared, Mama, someone would hear
my trembling voice and know I was alone."

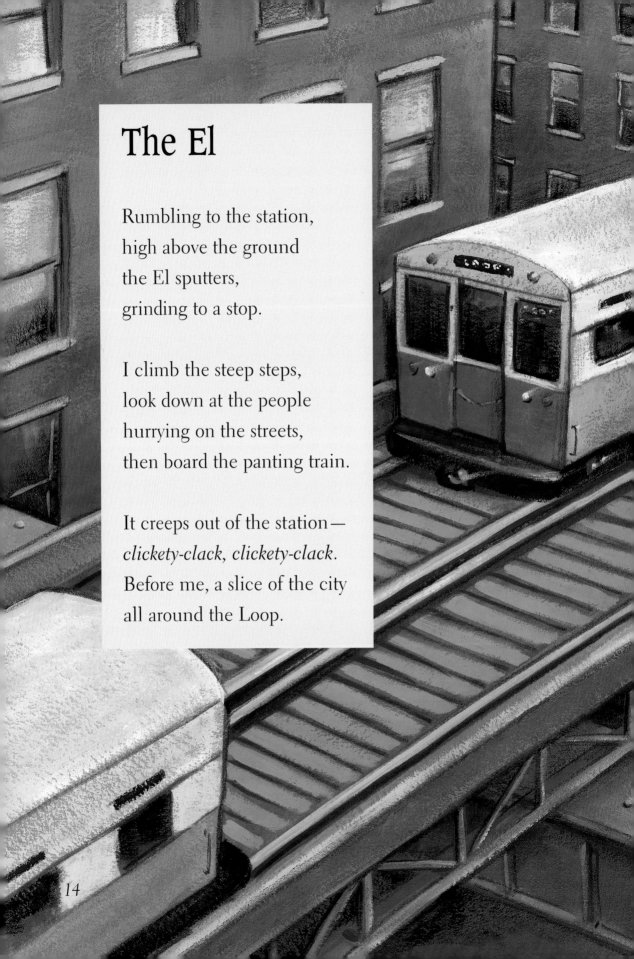

The El

Rumbling to the station,
high above the ground
the El sputters,
grinding to a stop.

I climb the steep steps,
look down at the people
hurrying on the streets,
then board the panting train.

It creeps out of the station—
clickety-clack, clickety-clack.
Before me, a slice of the city
all around the Loop.

The Subway

In my village
they dig underground,
build a water tank,
find a limestone quarry,
or bury those passed on.
Here in the city,
they dig underground,
lay subway lines—
crisscrossing spider webs,
where speeding trains carry
millions to work or play
all night, all day.

Washington, D.C.

My dream
to live the history
of my new country
takes flight in April,
when cherry blossoms
in fragrant dress
capture more eyes
than the monuments
raised for posterity.
The White House glistens
in all its brightness.
The Washington Monument
stands at attention,
saluting all who pass by.
At the Lincoln Memorial
I hear
Marian Anderson sing
"My country 'tis of thee."
I see thousands gathered
to hear Martin Luther King say,
"I have a dream."
And my own dream
comes true.

My First Symphony Concert

Under summer stars,
the symphony orchestra
performs an evening
of Beethoven.
The music surrounds me,
a sea of haunting melodies.
The violins, cellos,
and piano spill over me
in waves of wonder.
I leave humming
Beethoven's *Für Elise*,
instead of a reggae tune
I know so well.
I thought steel drums
were the best
till I heard
a hundred instruments
blend in harmony
under the conductor's baton.

Cathedral

I enter the church
in awe,
the most grand
I ever saw.
Stained-glass windows,
glistening jewels
in the sunlight.
Organ pipes stand like soldiers,
lift music to gothic spires
that scrape the skies.
Statues of saints
bless all who enter.
In my village church
I remember the Sunday sermon.
Inside this cathedral
I take away only memories
of wonder,
nothing of the sermon.

The Park

Midst the bustle
of the city
and a canopy
of concrete and steel,
I yield when the park beckons:
bidding me
rest awhile
in the breeze
of shade trees,
ride a bike
round the lake,
stroll the grounds —
like the green pasture
I roamed at home —
or just sit and talk
with friends
in the park.

New to the Big Top

Music explodes.
Excitement bubbles
through the crowd.
The world's greatest show
begins.
A fantasy flight is mine.
My eyes flash
from ring to ring—
trapeze artists fly,
daredevils walk on slim wires,
acrobats flip,
jugglers toss and catch,
tigers leap
through fiery hoops.
So much to see,
I need a dragonfly's
searchlight eyes
to zoom in on all three rings
under the big top tonight.

Amusement Park Adventure

In a crowd,
walking the boardwalk,
eating cotton candy,
licking my sticky fingers.

Rocketing high
on the roller coaster,
diving low,
eyes shut tight,
hiding my fear.
My braids fly,
heart pounds,
stomach trembles.

Circle round, circle round
on the Ferris wheel,
a dizzying whirl.
My screams of delight
mingle with others.

These new thrills,
my swirl in space,
linger long after
I leave the park.

23

The Library

I pass between lions
guarding what's inside:
bound gems to open,
endless words that sparkle.
I read till my eyes grow
leaden with sleep.

In my village,
Grandpa's well-used Bible
was the only book I knew.
I reread the stories,
could recite each one
like the poems I learned.

The Museum

Artists, the gift givers,
paint what they see,
what they feel.
Their passion explodes
in brushstrokes
to create landscapes
and portraits
that speak to me.
At the museum,
I linger over these treasures
by El Greco, Velázquez,
Gauguin, van Gogh,
mount them in my mind,
richer for their gifts.

Clothesline Friends, or Before E-mail

The courtyard's between us,
so Tess and I walk
up five flights of stairs
to visit and talk.

We hate to climb steps
and soon find a way
to visit each other
anytime of the day.

The clothesline between us
we use to pin notes.
We reel in the message
that each of us wrote.

We stand at our window,
and wave a quick sign.
We've just shared our secrets
on the backyard clothesline.

Skeleton Trees

I heard
of trees that shed
their autumn leaves—
yellow, orange, red—
before winter's snow.
But till I saw
those bony skeletons
without their leafy skins,
I never dreamed
trees would stand
like Halloween ghosts,
trembling in the wind.

28

Change of Clothes

At the edge of the ocean,
sea breezes filtered through
my flimsy muslin dress.
I felt buoyed up—
my wish to glide
like a butterfly.

Now in America,
wrapped in winter's warm woolens,
muffled with scarf and mittens—
nose almost frostbitten—
my wish to hibernate
like a cuddly bear.

First Snow

Outside my window
powdery flakes
fall, fall,
wrapping the ground
in soft cotton sheets,
dressing bare trees
in frozen lace
they never wore at home.
This winter miracle
lures me outside,
a timid fawn,
where my new boots sink,
leaving bold footprints
in my first snow.

My America

From a small fishing village,
on days without a catch to sell,
my dreams beyond Pa's canoe
lifted me on waves of longing.

I heard about a land where
hope glows, a beacon,
guiding ocean-deep dreamers
from storm surfs to shore.

I sailed to this promise,
landed in my chosen bay;
found shells to open, hopes to fill
in America, my new home.